LEO THE LOP

Written By:
STEPHEN COSGROVE
Illustrated By:
ROBIN JAMES

ISBN #0-915396-16-5 LEO THE LOP

P.O. Box 707
Bothell, Washington 98011

Dedicated to Wendy James, the memory of the real Leo the Lop and a filly called Flutterby.

In a warm, gentle corner of a soft, green forest a whole bunch of bunnies were born. There were so many baby rabbits, you almost wouldn't believe it. There were white ones, brown ones, even some with spots, and every one of them had a little pink nose, fluffy white tail, and two pointed ears that stood straight up in the air.

All of them, that is, except Leo the Lop.

Now it wasn't that Leo didn't have a little nose or a fluffy tail, for he did. What he didn't have was ears that stood straight up in the air. Instead of standing up, they hung straight down. That really didn't matter to Leo because he thought he was just as normal as could be. Besides, he couldn't see his ears anyway.

Day by day as the rabbits got older, they began to notice that Leo was slightly different. The more they looked at him, the funnier it seemed. It got so bad that the entire burrow of bunnies would roll on the ground holding their sides in fits of laughter every time Leo walked by.

You've got to admit that a rabbit walking around with his ears dragging in the dirt is pretty funny.

Now Leo was very confused. He didn't see anything so funny about the way he looked. His fur was the same. His tail was the same. As far as Leo was concerned he was perfectly normal.

Finally, out of frustration he asked, "How come you guys are always laughing at me?"

For a moment the other rabbits tried to be serious but they just couldn't hold back the laughter. One of the rabbits finally blurted out, "Your ears, you dope! They drag on the ground. You just aren't normal!"

Leo looked down and, sure enough, there were his ears dangling in the dust.

I guess Leo was kind of hurt. He really didn't feel any different than the other rabbits, but because his ears hung down instead of up, he just wasn't normal.

"Hmmmm!" he thought. "All I need is to exercise a little bit and my ears will stand up just like all the normal rabbits." So, with that in mind he struggled and strained, trying to make them stand up. Unfortunately the best he could do was to get them to stick straight out, and he could do that for only a minute. Then no matter how hard he tried they would flop back to the ground in a puff of dust.

"Well!" thought Leo, "That didn't work. Maybe, if I show my ears which way to go, they'll get the idea and go there on their own."

Very carefully he climbed a tree and, after cautiously hooking his hind legs around the branch, he dangled over upside down. Sure enough his ears hung straight down.

Leo must have hung that way for nearly an hour when a voice made him look around.

"Whatcha doin' that for?" spoke the voice.

Leo looked around and there, right before him, hanging from another branch, was a possum.

"Well," said Leo, feeling a little foolish, "I'm hanging upside down so my ears will learn which way they're supposed to go, so I can be a normal rabbit."

"What's normal?" asked the possum. "Before, when I saw you on the ground, your ears looked normal. Now they look upside down."

Leo thought and thought, and you know he didn't have an answer.

So with a flip he dropped to the ground. "Hmmm!" he thought, "If my ears going down are normal, then the other rabbits with their ears going up aren't normal. The more he thought about the other rabbits, the funnier it became. With a laugh and a giggle he raced off to tell them what he had discovered.

In bursts of laughter he told the other rabbits what he had found out. At first they didn't know whether to believe him, and then they started to look at one another and realized that Leo could be right.

"Oh dear! What are we going to do?" they cried.

"I've got an idea," said one of the rabbits. He picked up two big rocks and with some twine he tied them to the ends of his ears. Sure enough, with all that weight his ears began to droop lower and lower until they reached the ground.

Seeing his success, the other rabbits ran around picking up rocks and tying them to their ears.

Everything would have been all right except for one small problem: the rocks and ears kept getting all tangled up in tails and feet till all was confusion — with bunnies lying in a dusty heap.

"This isn't going to work!" they said. "There has got to be a better way."

"Maybe," said a little furry bunny, "If we showed our ears the way they should be normally, they would go that way naturally."

So, they all very carefully climbed a tree, and after tying their ears to the branch, they gently hooked their legs and swung over, hanging upside down. Sure enough, every one of those bunnies ears hung up instead of down.

They must have hung that way for a long time when a voice made them look around.

"Whatcha doin' that for? asked the voice.

They looked, and right before them, hanging from a branch, was that very same possum.

"Well," they said, feeling a little dumb, "We're hanging this way so our ears will be normal like Leo's."

"What's normal?" asked the possum. "Before, when I saw you all on the ground, your ears looked normal. Now they look upside down."

They all thought and thought, and you know, they couldn't answer the question either.

Carefully they untied their ears, and flip flopped to the ground below.

The rabbits thought and thought. "If we're normal and Leo is normal, then normal is whatever you are!" With a hop and a giggle, they raced off to tell Leo what they had learned.

After listening to their story, Leo had to agree that normal is whatever you are, and from that day forward the rabbits of the burrow lived very normal lives in the soft, warm forest.

SO, IF YOU ARE A RABBIT AND YOUR EARS GO UP OR DOWN, TRY TO REMEMBER LEO AND THE LESSON THAT HE FOUND.

Leo did still have one small problem . . .

His ears always drooped in his
soup.

level 3.5   .5 pt.
disk D-10
test 7524